R. H. (Richard H.) Horne

Prometheus the Fire Bringer

R. H. (Richard H.) Horne

Prometheus the Fire Bringer

ISBN/EAN: 9783744784474

Printed in Europe, USA, Canada, Australia, Japan

Cover: Foto ©Andreas Hilbeck / pixelio.de

More available books at **www.hansebooks.com**

PROMETHEUS

THE FIRE-BRINGER

BY

RICHARD HENRY HORNE

"AUTHOR OF ORION," &c., &c., &c

EDINBURGH

EDMONSTON AND DOUGLAS

1864

DEDICATION

TO

Dr. Leonhard Schmitz, Ph.D.,

&c., &c., &c.

Dear Friend of "Auld lang syne,"

Permit me to associate with your name he only poetical work I have offered to the public ince my residence in Australia,—a period now xtended over twelve strangely eventful years.

Bearing in mind your high and well-deserved repute for learning,—that you have been the specially chosen educator of several members of our present Royal Family (which, indeed, I do not mention on account of the royalty, but because the honor was conferred upon you by the wish of the late Prince Consort, one of the most elaborately educated and accomplished men of this age), and that your pen has contributed so many articles of profound research, in ancient Greek and Roman literature and art, to the great standard works of reference of the day ; I should never have ven-

tured to present this book to you, nor, perhaps, to
have attempted its composition, but for the recollection of the opinion you gave—when, some
fourteen years ago, I submitted to you the rough
draft of the design—that " it was conceived in
the true spirit of the ancient Greek tragic drama,
and especially of Æschylus." How I have filled
up that outline, it now remains for yourself, and
others qualified like you, to determine. I submit
the work—possibly my last—to the " fit audience"
who are admirers of the most ancient, as the
highest class of tragic drama,—and I do this with
the most profound and unaffected respect and
deference. The humility may easily be regarded
as perfectly sincere, and not the less so from the
fact of its being the only public occasion on which
I have ever expressed such a feeling.

Criticism is never disarmed by the plea of anta-
gonistic or untoward circumstances of any kind,—
and *rightly*, it is not, and never should be ;—but
I may ask of private friendship to bear with some
matters of detail, which a civilized position in life
would have easily enabled me to correct and im-
prove. I do not allude to the occasional want of
external finish, and the high polish now given to
the verses of such poets as my old friends Robert
Browning, and the Laureate ; nor to a certain
rugged form of expression, and a matter of fact
directness in the presentation of things " of the
earth, earthy," for all *that* is left rough-hewn in-

tentionally ; but to those errors which may have been committed, and left, from a want of means of reference to learned authors, or to Greek antiquities.

In this savage solitude—this Blue Mountain of dark forests, rains, and hurricanes—(a region, nevertheless, which may, some day, suddenly become a wildly populous field of gold-miners)—without books—without any society—impressed, at times, with a sense of the precariousness of human life, amidst horse-accidents, the fall of massive trees, or the evil chances of dark nights in localities abounding in waterholes and deep mining shafts in unexpected places, always left quite unprotected,—this Lyrical Drama was composed, in the intervals of labours of a very different kind, and written for the most part during the night. When completed, and copied with very great care, the manuscript was entrusted to a faithful, but not infallible hand (at least, as to the bridle hand) and it was lost, in mist or bog, or got astray somewhere ; so that I had to reproduce the entire MS. from my first rough draft, notes, old maps, and fragments, "against time," and under other circumstances more adverse than those attending its first composition. The labour was a high and hopeful pleasure to me, in the first instance ; but this unexpected pressure tried the temper of the metal severely. You now have the honest, undisguised egotism of the whole. Pray pardon it.

But completed the labour was, and within the special period; and I now lay it in the shadow of the statue of Æschylus—the shadow of his feet —in hopes that you, and other profound admirers of the ancient Greek tragic drama, will not only take it up forgivingly, as to the ambition, but with some feeling of sympathy and generous interest.

I am, my dear friend,

With the highest esteem and regard,

Yours always,

R. H. Horne.

Blue Mountains,
        Australia, 1864.

NOTE.

As it is impossible to know into whose hands a book, of any class, may chance to fall, and as it is very certain that many persons of the highest intelligence, taste, and feeling, have had no opportunities for the study of classical antiquities, I hope to be excused for offering a word or two on the nobly suggestive old fable of " Prometheus."

The Supreme Ruler of the Early Gods, at a very remote period of the Greek mythology, was Ouranos. His son "Iapetus" (Japetus) was one of the Titans, and the father of the Titan demi-god, Prometheus. Hence, the descendants of Ouranos were called the " Ouranidai." Of this early dynasty was also Oceanus, and his daughters the Sea-Nymphs, or Oceanides.

"Iapetus," with others of the Ouranidai, warred against Heaven, and dethroned the Ruling Power who succeeded Ouranos; but they were themselves vanquished by ZEUS (in later centuries adopted into the Roman mythology as *Jupiter*, or *Jove*), with the assistance of ATHENA (the *Minerva* of the Romans), and HEPHAISTOS, or *Vulcan*. APHRODITE was transferred into the Roman mythology under the name of *Venus*, and HELIOS, under that of *Phœbus*, or the *Sun-God*.

The common-place vulgar statement that Prometheus " stole fire" from Heaven, does no justice to the real spirit of this magnificent mythological fable. The expression would be better suited to the brutal prostitution of the popular taste for burlesquing, with prodigal costliness, the noblest and the most beautiful subjects. The Supreme Ruler, Zeus, did not take away the unspeakable blessing of *fire* from mortals. This severe punishment had been inflicted by the Ruling Power of an earlier period. But Zeus refused to restore the precious gift; and Prometheus undertook to obtain it for mankind. This great act of self-devotion brought down upon himself the most tremendous and long-lasting vengeance of Zeus. According to my view, Prometheus should therefore be regarded as the friend and instructor of Humanity,--its first Champion, and its first Martyr; — the grand old Pagan archetype, and providential foreshadowing of the Divine Master who came upon the earth many centuries afterwards.

R. H. H

ATHENA.

HEPHAISTOS.

APHRODITE.

PROMETHEUS.

ECHO.

CHORUS......
{
1. Sub-Chorus of Islanders.
2. Sub-Chorus of Shipwrecked Mariners.
3. Sub-Chorus of Troglodytes.
4. Sub-Chorus of OCEANIDES.
}

The Scene is at the foot of Mount Ætna.

The time, from day-break till mid-noon.

ERRATA.

Circumstances. to which allusion has been made in the Dedication, will account for, and, it is hoped, in some degree excuse the following Errata. They are in no respect the fault of the printer.

Page 12, line 21, for *Divine*, read *Thine own*
— 13 — 17, for *thy mystic spell*, read *thy spell*
— 18 — 11, for *towards*, read *tow'rds*
— 21 — 22, for *Yes*, read *But*
— 29 — 1, for *glistening*, read *streaming*
— 33 — 19, for *Our course*, &c., read *We cried to the Gods, but our course*, &c.
— 34 — 15, for *grand*, read *great*
— 35 — 10, for *will*, read *shall*
— ,, — 12, for *sylvan*, read *sacred*
— ,, — 21, for *this morning's*, read *the morning's*
— 40 — 6, for *form*, read *limbs*
— 43 — 4, for *path more*, read *pathway*
— 46 — 15, for *mad*, read *wrong*
— 47 — 1, for *our sea-green eyes*, read *our eyes*.
— ,, — 12, for *And trample us into*, read *And scatter our lives in*
— 49 — 15, for *as before!* read *as before,*
                        So he be pardon'd. Lead him not away!
— 50 — 6. for *At the bottom of*, read *On the plains beneath*
— ,, — 10, for *profoundest depths*, read *depths of emerald*
— ,, — 17, for *the coral*, read *glimm'ring*
— 53 — 8. for *With frost-white flowers*, &c., read
                        Among the white crags seated high
— ,, — 9, *In that petrific air;*
— ,, — 10, *Low chanting many a prophesy*
— ,, — 11, *Of hope enrich'd by memory.*

PROMETHEUS THE FIRE-BRINGER.

ATHENA.

BENEATH this island's lowest granite rocks
And heated porphyry, I hear thy voice
Break the divine star-silence of the night,
O, Hundred-handed Giant whom I slew,
By my war-chariot clad with blazing swords,
Rushing amidst thy limbs, and buried here,
To groan beside black Typhon. Thou would'st taunt me
With change of mind, and treachery to Zeus,
Since I befriend Prometheus, who designs
To save the human race, as thou hast heard.
But Destiny, throughout all Nature, frames
Wise laws of change by infinite degrees,
And modes, and times ; and I from Father Zeus
Am only moved as star removes from star,—
Retaining our relations. By his brain—
Which, brain-like, is but half in self-control—
Teeming with fresh creations, and the power
To call them forth in substances and forms,
And for his further views—perchance some fears,
Beyond thy thought—he contemplates to sweep
Mankind from off the earth, replacing them
By a different race. Fruitless annihilation !
Prometheus, the far-seeing, knows that men,
In any shape on earth, will still be men,
And hence would them preserve, and from their state
Of present want and misery redeem.
Wherefore, O, smouldering Giant, lie thou still

Beneath this island's ever-trembling crags,
And think not any aid I may accord
Prometheus, 'gainst the Ruler of the Gods,
Will reach to thee.   I am the same I was ;
Like Nature, with due course of difference.
But now the stars retire ! and Mother Night,
With a profound sigh, heard by Gods alone,
And understood by only some of them,
Shade after shade withdraws ; while down the slope
Of dusky Ætna, a more dusky form
Descends.   It is Hephaistos from his forge !

HEPHAISTOS.

Wise, war-surpassing Goddess, thou hast heard,
As I have heard, the struggles and the voice
Of the deep-buried one, Enkelados,
Who, by some chance, has been apprised of deeds
Prometheus contemplates, and thinks once more
To come on earth, for battles as of old,
Against Olympos' King.   But what, indeed,
Would Atlas' brother, forewarn'd, rashly do ?

ATHENA.

He hath not spoken it, but by my knowledge
Of superhuman, as of human thoughts,
I do perceive he hath resolved to save
Mankind from Zeus' destroying hand.

HEPHAISTOS.
                        What means
Hath he to do this ?

ATHENA.
                        Bring them back the glory
Of earthly things, man once possessed, by Fire !

HEPHAISTOS.
The flower and glory also of the Gods !
This were rebellion, and it must not be.

Son of the Titans, he would once again
Call up a race to crush our several thrones !
But see, the wretched Islanders approach !

ATHENA.

They creep like shades before the coming day ;
But the fair day will come, and man look up.
And others also come from foreign shores,—
With Sea-Nymphs, following slowly, as in thought.

The Four Divisions of the CHORUS *march on, in slow time,
and form.*

CHORUS.

Grey, silent twilight of the dawn !
How often have we watched in vain,
On lone sea sands, or fields of weedy corn,
Or barren stony plain,
The coming of a season less forlorn,
When life, like day, would rise again.

SUB-CHORUS THE FIRST.

[*Islanders.*]

But mornings creep and climb
Above our miserable heads ;
Their course is marked no more than shell-fish slime,—
We sink in ignorance to our earthy beds.
We strive to till the soil,
And weeds, or blight, or rotting grain,
Reward our toil.

SUB-CHORUS THE SECOND.

[*Shipwrecked Mariners.*]

We strive to sail across the main :
We drive on rocks where billows boil !

Sub-Chorus the Third.

[*Troglodytes.*]

Our dwelling is in holes and caves :
We seem to live within our graves.

Sub-Chorus the First.

While he who tries to build, soon finds
Some mad, mane-tossing Winds,
From Boreas' echoing stalls,
Bear far away his roof—lay flat his walls !

Sub-Chorus the Fourth.

[*Oceanides.*]

If omens come, man cannot read them ;
If saviour gods, man does not heed them :
Because his eyes can only see
His body's wants and misery.
The few who have a clearer sight
Are folded in the common night ;
For all, with purblind dreams o'ergrown,
Mistake clear vision for their own.
Thou, great Athena, know'st our kinsman's plan ;
Protect, and aid, the heroic Friend of Man !

Choragus.

O, Goddess, if thy presence here
    Betoken good to human kind,
Address some words to us ! O, come more near,
    That we may take into each sense
    Divine ambrosial influence,
      In body, and in mind ;
And learn if any happy chance
    May better this our fallen state,
Though dark Hephaistos frowns askance,
    Reminding us of Zeus and Fate !

CHORUS.

Grey, purpling twilight of the dawn !
    Thou changest softly in thy hues ;
    Sad-coloured orange melting streaky blues,
Show that another infant Day is born.

ATHENA.

Be hopeful.   Nothing on the mythic earth,
However low—a rudiment of life—
That once uplifts its head into the light,
Retains its meanness, but begins to climb ;
Receiving *that*, in modified due course,
Which soon will be caught down, *at once* from Heaven.

SUB-CHORUS THE FIRST.

Thy words, O Goddess, pass beyond
    The measure of our thought ;
    But with some purport they are fraught,
Which teaches man should ne'er despond.

CHORUS.

Retiring twilight of the dawn !
    A coming radiance through thee glows ;
The rapture of thy mystic spell is gone,
    Transforming slowly, like an opening rose !

ATHENA.

Receive the omen !—something is at hand
Of highest good for Man, if he will use
The gift aright.   Daughters of old Oceanus !
Lo ! where the burning breath and nostril-smoke
Of Helios' chariot steeds, from the eastern line
Begin to rise ! Soon will he clothe with light
The flat earth and its circumambient sea.
But ere the God of Day pass o'er your heads,
A daring act, worthy a Titan's son,
Will be attempted.

HEPHAISTOS.

And as surely punished.

CHORUS.

What act, O, Goddess! and what son,
Or great descendant of that ancient race,
Which in Olympos' highest place,
Once sat on thrones near the All-Ruling One?

HEPHAISTOS.

Beware of those unmeasured words! The reign
Of that old dynasty has long since ended;
And now the thunder from my sacred forge,
Vibrates in other hands.

CHORUS.

Yet, Goddess, say or show
What act—what Titan——?

SUB-CHORUS OF OCEANIDES.

Great Prometheus!
No other can it be, we know
From our hoar sire Oceanus,
Who sent us from his emerald caves below.

ATHENA.

Yes, it is he; and he would now restore
The greatest boon that mortals e'er possessed—
Their greatest loss—the Gods' first glory—Fire!

CHORUS.

What sudden gleams,
What blinding beams,
Break o'er our minds, and dazzle every thought!
As though we once had known
A blessing that had flown,—
A wonder vanished, leaving us distraught!

CHORAGUS.

Vague memories rise, and flit across—
As of a grandsire's dying words,
Which of *his* grandsire he records,—
So that we seem to know our unknown loss.

CHORUS.

But wherefore did some Ancient God's behest
That glorious gift withdraw,
Leaving a man no better than a beast ;
And why doth Zeus withhold afar ?

ATHENA.

Prometheus comes !—believe in him.   Farewell !

CHORUS.

'Midst folding mists of silver-grey,
The stately Goddess, on her car,
Rich in device of peace and war,
Brazen-winged griffins bear away !

HEPHAISTOS.

Welcome ! true son of great Iapetus—
Noblest of Titans, though his body lie
In Tartarus for ever.

PROMETHEUS.
Still, a God.
Hail, friend ! albeit I know thy hand can forge
Chains for a tyrant's vengeance, as of yore.

HEPHAISTOS.
But most unwillingly, at times, thou knowest.

CHORUS.
This is the God !
The Titan's son !
Who beareth the rod
Of the shining One !

To waive in the air,
Make want disappear,
And our life-course, clear
As the rivers, run !

PROMETHEUS.

Such rod of power I have not in my hand,
But I will strive to gain it, and restore
To suffering Man.

HEPHAISTOS.

Man is not worth the risk
Which you incur.   Ungrateful is the race,
By nature, more especially to those
Who serve them most, and sacrifice themselves.

PROMETHEUS.

That question forms no part of my design.
Full oft when man hath cause for gratitude,
Some gall-drops lie beneath, that he should need
Such service.   Yearnings for a vague perfection,
Fret the fine roots of his imperfect nature.
These poor beginnings of the human race,
Are centuries distant from such noble themes !
Therefore say nothing more of gratitude.

CHORUS.

Thou hast not, in thy present hold,
This glory, wondrous to behold,
Of powers and uses manifold,
Which once we had, as we are told :
But wherefore have we lost ?
What act—what thought, in young or old,
This dreadful penalty hath cost ?

HEPHAISTOS.

The Ruler of the Elder Gods withdrew
The spirit of power from mortals, for their crimes.

Sub-chorus of Oceanides.

Answer Choragus!—strike, from varied strings,
The sacred harmony of music's wings,
   Which goat-horn'd lyre,
   Cithara, harp and phormynx, now inspire!

Choragus.

That race is long extinct ; its debt,
   However deep, is deeply paid,
And Chronos, in his star-light net,
   Hath borne them to eternal shade.
Those mortals are to us no more
   Than wrecks beneath a fabled sea ;
Shells ground to sand, on some strange shore,
   Beyond the dreams of memory.
Then wherefore should the Reigning Power
   Invest our lives with serpent-rings,—
Call from the dust a weed, or flower,
   To bear the curse of unknown things ?

Hephaistos.

Shall the worm turn, and, midst its tiny coils,
Measure Eternity, and Zeus' decrees ?

Prometheus.

Honour the dynasty of the Early Gods !
Peace and fertility to the grass of mortals,
Who did and suffered in that grand old time.

Hephaistos.

And suffered justly.

Prometheus.

      Doubtfully, to reason.

Chorus.

Seeing, they did not make themselves,
But like the insects, trees, and flowers in season,

Came up—looked round—
Received the high Sun's passing smile—
Drooped—and sank back into the ground,
Like those who dwell upon this isle.

HEPHAISTOS.

The early race of men offended Heaven,
And were swept down.   It may be so again ;
And ye may find yourselves in Tartarus,
Like those before ye !

PROMETHEUS.

So—he stumbles off !
The great Artificer of the Gods, retires,—
Ascending zig-zag towards his lofty forge.
Mark now the actual business of the hour !
The marble quarry, and the granite rock,
Are solid masses of unshapely stone,
Till mind and hand the ponderous block inspire ;
Prepare ye therefore to receive a gift,
The greatest mortals ever can receive—
(Except those gifts they cannot comprehend),
One which shall give them skill and mastery
Over all metals, and all earthly forms ;—
For now I am prepared to scale the Heavens,
And bring down Fire, which Man shall keep for ever.

SUB-CHORUS OF OCEANIDES.

[*With lyre and phormynx.*]

Oh Titan God !
Descendant of the ancient Dignities !
The grand old Dynasty, whereof the Syrens
Sing to their star-entrancing lyres,
And Echo bears among the shining spheres,
For soft responses through Infinity !
Son of the father of the human race—

Iapetus !
Revered in surging tears by hoary Ocean,
Beloved by all his Daughters, and all spirits
That comprehend, or simply feel thy purpose,—
Thy pure, self-sacrifice, without our thought
That sacrifice of self is anything ;
Receive our prayers, our blessings, and our hearts,—
Not meanly, slavishly, but all in love,
Honour and Glory, Faith, Hope, full reliance,—
And now we wait to see thy perilous daring.

SUB-CHORUS, FIRST AND SECOND.

But, oh, Prometheus ! saviour of our race,
    Low-fallen—ever punished—pause awhile :
We are not all of self—not utterly base—
    Though God-abandoned, crawling on this isle ;
We can—we do, feel for thee, as ourselves.
And one who fishes, digs, and delves,
Hunts, tends his herds, for ever thus employed—
    In lowest needs, at once says all
    In rough words, like rough things let fall ;
And we implore thee not to be destroyed
By efforts for our good !—O, we are worth
    No sacrifice of noble earth,
    Far less of one so high.
This from our inmost life, we pray,—we cry !

PROMETHEUS.

That cry, from the deep well of human life,
Which would restrain, drives onward my resolve,
Sparkling my springs of being with the sense
Of a true common nature in the world.

CHORUS.

    Yet pause awhile !
    'Tis sunrise !—its alarming smile

Gilds every face, like demons in dismay !
Thou hopeful, yet too dreadful God of Day,
What dost thou bring ?
We tremble for ourselves !—for everything !

PROMETHEUS.

It is not yet the hour to light my torch :
I wait for the full blaze of Helios' car.

CHORUS.

Then wilt thou meet in their ascent,
The frantic, snow-white Horses of the Sun !
And, through the blinding element
Of flame-light, plunge to thy intent ;—
Bethink thee, ere the deed be done !

PROMETHEUS.

I have thought deeply ; and shall think no more,
Lest it disturb the action clearly planned.

CHORUS.

We tremble still—our fear is wise,
Having no knowledge of the skies—
Nor much of aught beneath that lies.

PROMETHEUS.

My sons, think what the earth hath lost thro' fear !

SUB-CHORUS THE FIRST.

What have we lost ?

SUB-CHORUS THE SECOND.

Good lives, sometimes—
When fear suspended active power—
By hand of man, or tooth of beast,
The falling tree, the snake beneath the flower ;

By floods, or snows in Scythian climes,
By lightning, or the crater-shower;
By sunken rocks in unknown seas;
By sudden darkness—strange disease.

SUB-CHORUS THE THIRD.

By hunger also, when stored food
Was in the land;
By want of clothing, till our blood
Ran cold about our bones,
Like winter-rills through stones,
While skins of goats were near at hand,
And sheep and oxen open to demand!
We feared to seize, though Nature's laws
Showed us just cause;
And feared to work, lest hire should be
A bait for daily slavery.

PROMETHEUS.

The earth is broad enough for each man's bread,
And work, no less than food, is necessary.
Only a slavish mind can be enslaved;
E'en though Olympos' Ruler crushed his form:
For tyrants thrive best on man's dreamy fears,
Thus liberty is lost. Fear groundless fears.

CHORUS.

Yes, we have lost so many things
Through fear, we tremble yet the more,
Lest hell-born powers with flaming wings
Should bear us to their native shore.

PROMETHEUS.

Into the future gazing, I perceive
Imagination works more influence
Than all man's other faculties combined;
Siding with indolence, and slackening nerve;

Arming and pluming Incapacity,
In those whose strong desire to have and hold,
Mistakes itself for efforts well applied,
And worthiness to win.   But oh, my sons,
What fear has lost in this rude twilight age,
Is nothing to the losses yet to come !
One thing I promise ye, it shall not cause
The loss of this commanding element
Ye need, for uses without number.

CHORUS.

Fire !
Shall we receive that wonder from thy hand ?

SUB-CHORUS THE FIRST.

We pray for things we do not understand !

PROMETHEUS.

I have promised it.   By means of this bright gift,
Most useful arts, unnumbered, as unknown
To present mortals, will be re-attained,
And gradually make perfect.   Brass and iron,
Will take the place of flint ; pulse, berries, roots,
Exchanged for well-stored grain.   Rude huts and caves
Will be transformed to homes of artful brick,
Made with baked mud and straw, or hewn from rocks ;
And graves of mariners to sheltering coves,
Where ships ride safe at anchor.   Bear in mind,
Your ancestors were taught by me to frame
And use the plough ; also to tame and manage
Poseidon's gift, left wild as his own waves—
Until Athena placed within my hands
A bridle ; and for oxen shaped the yoke,
Whereby with foreheads garlanded, and hymns
To the beneficent ægis-bearing Queen,
They turned the black soil upward to the sun,

Amidst her olive-groves. Elms, hung with vines
In long festoons, hoary with tasselled fruit,
And corn-fields flowing to the horizon's verge,
O'er level plain and softly swelling downs,
Were all as common blessings on the earth,—
Athena with her counsels aiding me.
Such things, and many others, swept away
With a past race, shall re-appear.

CHORUS.

With Fire !
Its spirit dawns like a new soul,
That sees a new course open, a new goal !

PROMETHEUS.

Quarrying and mining, will again become
The means of many triumphs. By the first,
Substance is gained for the Arch-builder's art,
Of widest usefulness and perennial grandeur ;
From humblest roof, to loftiest dome or spire,
Rough-hewn, or rich in statues of the Gods,
Where man can pour libations—offer up
His prayers with incense-fumes and dirging hymns,
While the blood bubbles o'er the gilded floor,
Ere the dark rites and mysteries begin ;—
Man's mad devices not approved by me :
And by the second, wealth incalculable,
Will shine o'er earth, which, wrongly used, will prove
A curse, but used aright, a means of good ;
Such good as, in a future age, the mines
Of silver-glittering Laurion will confer,
Whereby ten score black-bench'd triremes, by Greeks
Shall be constructed, and at once destroy
The invading bird-flocks of a Persian fleet,
Coming to rend the mind and chain the man,
Screaming down Art and Science at their birth—
Choking life's noblest waters at their source.

Sub-Chorus the First.

And without fire such things had never been,
As thou hast seen ;
Nor could they be,
As thy prophetic vision now doth see.

Chorus.

And can we touch this wonder in thy hand ?
What is it ?　Doth it live and feed ?
If so, 'were terrible indeed ;
If dead, how can it serve our need ?

Sub-Chorus the First.

We pray for things we do not understand.

Prometheus.

'Tis common in all temples ; but the good Gods
Reserve for their own wisdom what to grant.

Chorus.

We see it in the sun's great ball !
We see it in the lightning !
The moon and stars—the meteor's rushing fall—
The glow-worm's fitful brightening !
The crater's brief up-blazing tree !
The smitten night-wave's brilliancy !
The fly and beetle's many coloured lamp,
O'er dark old graves and dismal swamp,
Whose dews and fogs are death—inhaled, imbibed !
But how collect, coerce, combine—
The fitful flame-leaves intertwine,—
Of that out-shooting, luminous vine,
Thou hast erewhile described ?
How shall we hold
The flashing and aërial gold ?

How shall we act, so that it be
Ours, and obtain not mastery
O'er us, and all that we possess,—
A gift too great, that adds to our distress !

PROMETHEUS.

Possession mostly gives the power to use !
The man who first bestrode the fierce wild horse—
Curbed his frothed mouth—defied his bloodshot eye—
Caressed his high-arched neck, and taught his legs
To change their rampant bounds for regular pace,—
Slow—surging gracefully—or fleet as wind
That skims the desert with unruffled wing ;—
E'en such a man will learn to handle fire.
His tribe will follow.

CHORUS.

Thou hast done this thing,
    And wilt, again, with cheering smile ;
Teaching thy art so perilous
    Unto the worthiest on our isle,
Should'st *thou* attain it, O, Prometheus !
    But how can we,
Who comprehend no more than we can see,
    And nought of that, at times,
Conceive this arduous contest won,
    When each who up a mountain climbs,
Dares not too boldly face the sun,
While thou design'st to seize the solar fire ?

SUB-CHORUS THE FIRST AND THIRD.

If thy attempt should prove thy funeral pyre,
    How shall we bear
    The inclement wintry air,
    And our savage food and fare,
After so many hopes and dreams
Of earthly blessings from these subject beams ?

PROMETHEUS.

As I will bear my fate, so bear thou thine.

CHORUS.

But tell us more !
Oh, let us know
How thou wilt 'scape the cloudy roar
Of bolts from Zeus,—for swift or slow,
They will thy form in ashes strow,
And, with them, scatter all our hopes !
Show us thy aims, and ends—
Thy means—thy Titan friends—
Thy wall of shields—and towering ladder-slopes !

PROMETHEUS.

Too great an action fills my mind for words.
I cannot further speak.

SUB-CHORUS THE FIRST.

He turns aside—
Like one who knows the time and tide !
Straight onward moves, gathering a hollow reed—
A pine-bough, for a torch, beside !

SUB-CHORUS THE FIRST, SECOND, AND THIRD.

Will he indeed
Defy the power of Zeus, who hath denied
To man the use of this bright element ?
Can he succeed ?
Father of Gods, O give consent,
Even against thy first harsh will,
And let him fill,
From thy great fountain-glare, and bring
To earth the struggling luminous thing,
To warm our blood—
Encrease our food,—

Nor injuring fruit, or grain, or grass, --
To melt and model any mass—
Make tools of iron, copper, brass—
Darts, spears, and shields.

SUB-CHORUS FIRST.

See where Prometheus strides beyond the fields !

SUB-CHORUS OF OCEANIDES.

We weave our choral-dance, and pray,
But also fear the Gods have fixt a bound,—
Jealous of man's ascent beyond his clay,
Heavenward, and questioning Stars and Thrones around.
But, O Great Zeus ! if it may be,
Relent, and spare Humanity !
And leave its little scope quite free !

CHORUS.

See, where Prometheus strides the lowlands now !
Across the creeks and floods,—
Over the uplands steadfastly and slow !
And now into the darkling woods !
Mysterious caves are there,
Serpents, and dragons grim and spare,
Stone-shapes and Shadows, whispering ' Would'st thou dare ?'
But see ! above the sombre line
Of distant forest—cedar, pine—
Rises a head—human—divine—
And shoulder like the Appenine,
Looming afar !
But to our straining thoughts, a rising star
Where'on our eyes and hopes are fixed,
And gushing tears with aspirations mixed.

SUB-CHORUS OF OCEANIDES.

Oh, listen !—faintly breathing—
Wafting—swelling—swooning—stealing—

Æolian music 'tends the mystic wreathing
Of sapphire-glowing vapours, now revealing
    Prometheus' fast-ascending feet!

CHORUS.

'Tis followed by a different sound,
  Like silver trumpets under-ground!
It searches our hair-roots—so thrilling sweet!
    O, may that more than martial symphony
    Inspire the Titan's soul with victory!

SUB-CHORUS THE FIRST.

  What favoring Goddess' hand,
To sounds that make us tremble, yet exult,
Preluding a foreknown result,
    Works the invisible command,
Whereat yon shrouding mist of dazzling blue,
Melts the horizon in its violet hue,
So that the Hero's perilous ascent
From earth into the firmament,
He makes, unknown to the Olympian host?

CHORAGUS.
[*With cithara and phormynx.*]

Oh, can such hopes as these be lost?
    Can such exalted dreams be vain,
    Falling like Hesperidean rain
  Of liquid gold and emerald pale,
      Calling forth flowers
      For Goddess' bowers,
To end like thistle-down upon the gale?
    Cheering the heart of future-seeking man,
    By nourishing his fancy's span
With fruit too high, which no one can attain?

SUB-CHORUS OF OCEANIDES.

We heard Athena's trumpets sound
  Beneath the ecstatic and uplifting ground!

And now our glistening locks receive
A fragrance, such as fumes of incense give,
When from rough jasper cups libations pour,
Propitiating Gods on high ;
For lo ! another Deity
Approaches !—Aphrodite ! loveliest flower
Of Ocean, Earth, and of Olympos' sky !

CHORUS.

Hail Goddess ! too divinely fair
For mortal vision, and earth's heavy air !
Spell-bound we stand—scarcely to breathe we dare !

APHRODITE.

The luminous gold of Helios' floating reins
Erewhile I saw amidst the breaks of cloud,
And soon Prometheus will a brother meet,
Whose course is fixed by an eternal law,
And may not favour any other scheme.
The Sun hath his own system ; and the rays
For Earth allotted cannot be encreased,
Or lessened, save by some Titanic act,
Which may bring down destruction.   Still, believe
Wisdom and Love make all things possible.

CHORUS.

Amidst the orient clouds we see
The beautiful gleam
Of the golden-floating reins,
And the radiating beam
On the upper plains,
Reflecting the Sun-God's pageantry !

APHRODITE.

O, not in vain your Hero scales the Heavens,
For time may be divided infinitely,
And actions in the period of a thought—
A single flash—a ray—one spark intense—

May dart forth, changing thus the destiny
Of Earth, and all that on her surface moves.
Hephaistos, not at heart an envious God,
But friendly to the Titan, is firm-clench'd
In his allegiance to his Father, Zeus,
And cannot act, or think, in adverse ways.
It is an honoured God, whom I am bound
To know as one that claims me for his own ;
But I, perceiving human elements
Have some divinity perversely mixed
In their creation, never can forego
Belief and hope of man's refining change,
From Egypt's dusky-leaved aureola,
To a new series worthy Heaven's best care :
Psyche, from coarsest substances evolved—
Passing through passion's trials—earthly wrongs
Self-contradictions purified in fire—
And human love, in its full human sense,
Made perfect, to the honour of the hand
That moulded and inspirited his clay.
This, sons of earth, and Daughters nobly born
Of the divine, foam-crown'd Oceanus,
I, Aphrodite, Goddess of the fount,
The germ, root, spirit, essence of sentient life—
The only life of limitless advance,
Or, bounded only by the spheric laws—
To you declare, and breathe into your hearts
The hope and confidence of that success
Man may not merit, but shall yet receive,
Because we know—Athena and myself—
That poor humanity, in every clime,
Hath never had fair dealing from his Gods.

Echo.

"Too lenient to his crimes !
" His crimes ! his crimes !

" 'Tis man's own fault!
" His fault!—his crimes!"

CHORUS.

Some direful Voice, faint Echo hither wafts!
Whose Voice?—The earth shakes underneath our feet!
From the volcano's smoking gloom it came!

SUB-CHORUS THE SECOND.

1. Let us haste to the sea shore!
2. Hoist sail!—ply the oar!
3. And wait not for wind or for tide!
4. Our faults, and our crimes,
   In many distant climes,
   Pursue us o'er the waters wide!
5. Beshrew craft and crew—
   Both by sea and land, undo!
6. And pursue us o'er the waters wide!

APHRODITE.

Hephaistos spake—but not to you his words.
Who are these strangers?

CHORAGUS.

Shipwrecked mariners!

SUB-CHORUS THE SECOND.

O, Cytheræan Goddess, and Protectress!

APHRODITE.

Whence come ye, friends?

SUB-CHORUS THE SECOND.

1. From many a shore
   We never had beheld before,
2. And ne'er shall visit any more.
3. All ignorant, but adventurous men.
4. Fragments of many a wreck are we.
5. Phœnician and Pelasgian.
6. What should we know of sailing thro' the sea?

APHRODITE.

What shores ?—what seas ?—your briny wanderings tell.

SUB-CHORUS THE SECOND.

We braved the broad Ionian surge,
From hundred-citied Creta's coast,
Where great King Phasmos launched a fleet,
Which did rare deeds, and then was lost.

APHRODITE.

Where gain'd your bark safe shelter from the storms?

SUB-CHORUS THE SECOND.

O, Goddess ! upon Afric's coast,
Like shells and shingles we were cast,
And tow'rds Betzura shaped our way,
As naked as a new-made mast.
But in that stately tower-wall'd mound,
Most hospitable cheer we found.

APHRODITE.

Where next, ye heedless children of the wave ?

SUB-CHORUS THE SECOND.

Thence, soon again, with songs and flags,
We bore a cargo o'er the deep,
To Scythian lands, and on the crags
Of Salmydessia's foaming jaws
Had nearly sunk to lasting sleep.
What should we know of sailing through the sea ?
Or travelling inland ?—ignorant men are we.
We left our bark ;—away we sped,
Hearing of gold mines—vein and seam—
Common as lead !
Foot-torn we wandered, till we saw
The Arimaspian mountains gleam
In the white distance !   'Twas a dream !
The gold was in a crazy head.

APHRODITE.

And thence, how came ye here?

SUB-CHORUS THE SECOND.

We found, at length, our best-loved element—
    The old, inconstant, dashing sea—
And on some new adventure bent,
    Into its billowy breast dashed we.
On prosperous gales we bore away
    With a good freight of furs and oil,
Till anchor'd in Aulonia's bay
    We were paid well for our slight toil.
Thence, caught by squalls, we sighted tracks
    Along the Locrian sea-board lying,
But fled adrift in sail-rent plight,
    Like leeward birds who scream while flying.
For days and nights we curs'd and prayed
    Alternately and constantly ;
Exhausted—yet to sleep afraid—
What should we know of sailing through the sea?
    A new moon came:
    Our course held the same!

APHRODITE.

The Sun moves upward !—quickly to the end !

SUB-CHORUS THE SECOND.

We knew not whither we scudding sped,
Till broken waters we spied ahead,
And then too clearly we saw our course—
The end of this cruize—with the chance of a worse !
A shifty wind, and a leeward draught,
Made our helmsman look like a child on a raft;
Our rudder unshipp'd—the rigging scatter'd—
Our mad bark struck—and her bows were shatter'd,
While the rent sail flank'd in the flagging breeze,
On the reefs of the Argyraspides.

c

APHRODITE.

But wherefore came ye here ?—or by what chance ?
If ye know clearly, speak it not too plain.

SUB-CHORUS THE SECOND.

O, Goddess, 'tis within our brains
Confused, as eye-sight when it rains.
Another craft received us straight—
Such as survived that last ill-fate—
And, one and all, we vowed to be
More pious towards the Gods, and thee !
One night our captain had a dream :
 A shrill voice from the eastward came,
Which cried " Ortygia ! "—and next morn,
 We found we all had dreamed the same.
And every night for thrice three nights,
 Right in the path of the morning star,
'Midst the black clouds we saw grand sights !
Torch-Races !—with fast flashing lights,
 And shrilling cries—" Ortygia ! "
Before our eyes new demi-gods had birth,
Which, from the saffron robes of Eos' breast came forth !
And then the Sun glode down, and kissed the Earth !

APHRODITE.

No more. The moment— and the act—draw near !

SUB-CHORUS THE SECOND.

Oh, from that night great joy had we,
While flying through the singing sea—
Its foaming, hissing, laughing white and blue,
Following in leaping rows behind !
Some Goddess sent a faithful wind—
The first we ever knew !

ECHO.

" Some Goddess sent—
We ever knew ! "

APHRODITE.

Peace ! thou unnatural child of Earth and Air !

CHORUS.

The patient shepherd folds his flock ;
    The weary mariner stows his spars ;
Then, purposeless, on deck or rock,
    Watch for the rise, or setting of the stars.
But we are taught that nobler things
    By active knowledge may be won ;
Two Goddesses expand broad wings,
    Tipt with the fire-gold of the Sun,
    And point to deeds that will be done !

SUB-CHORUS OF OCEANIDES.

Gone !—Aphrodite melts and fades,
Like summer lights in sylvan glades !
    And in the air
    Around—afar—
    Float odours rare
Of flowery isles—incense—ambrosia !

CHORUS.

    And we are left, expecting still
    Triumphant signs—

SUB-CHORUS OF OCEANIDES.

        Or signs of ill !

CHORAGUS.

Prepare the embattled Choral Dance,
    In honour of this morning's birth,
Whereon for prosperous advance,
    A sudden change comes o'er the earth !
While phormynx, and cithara strings
    Mingle with varied voices sweet,

Evolve, from east to west, your martial wings,—
    Then back return with measured feet.
Resume the Dance, from west to east,
    The second strophe's chorus-song—
The second anti-strophe next,
    Back to the centre brings your throng.
Full in the centre then whirl round—
    Your phalanx-dance—the epode's verse—
And add the wild flute's double sound,
    Man's future ages to rehearse.

CHORAL-DANCE.

S. 1st.

In our night-time,—
    Deep darkness !
        Our day-path,
            As markless—
                Our life's hearth
                    As sparkless,
                Man was like his own shade

A.S. 1st.

                    For he knew not
                His measure,—
            His hard lot,
        Or treasure,—
     His plague-spot,
   Or pleasure,—
        Were by himself made.

S. 2nd.

But from twilight,
    This morning,
        God and Goddess
            Gave warning,—
                Hope's fresh beams
                Adorning
        Our land and our sea

A.S. 2ND.

>> For the Titan
>> Is earning
>> A victory
>> Burning ;
>> Our destinies
>> Turning,
>> To make the slave free !

E.

>> Then whirl round,
>> With tramp and bound!
>> 'Tis Prometheus' chosen ground
>> Our Dance-Chorus tread !
>> Let shrill pipe, and magic string
>> With varied voices mingle,
>> Cymbals clash, and sweetly tingle,
>> Or sharply ring and ding,
>> Until ye wake the dead !

1.
>> Rouse and shift,
>> And then lift
>> Your dank and dusky head !
>> Forth ! come forth, O, ye dead !

2.
>> Lo ! a prize,
>> From the skies !
>> So, from mound and mouldering bed,
>> And cold, wreck-rich sand,
>> Come forth, O, ye dead !
>> And 'midst our Phalanx stand !

3.
>> But if ye can awake
>> And your old place take,
>> We shall know ye were never really dead ;
>> Though common dust ye seemed,
>> Ye will be what prophets dreamed,
>> By Prometheus' torch redeemed
>> From your Lethean bed !

CHORUS.

For the Titan now will bring,
    All struggling from the skies,
The ecstatic, flashing thing,
    To arm with light the hand and head,
    And glorify the eyes !

SUB-CHORUS OF OCEANIDES.

Reserve your comos—your exulting joys—
    Until a fitting hour;
For now, perchance, the God of Light destroys
    The self-devoting Hero's power!

SUB-CHORUS THE FIRST.

Whatever stars arise,
Seem adverse to perverted eyes !

SUB-CHORUS THE SECOND.

Whatever shore they find
Is a reef, with a foul wind !

SUB-CHORUS THE THIRD.

And our caves, when warm and high,
Are the beds where serpents lie !

CHORAGUS.

Like a child that lies on its mother's breast,
Mankind will sleep, and smile at rest,
    While the earthquake heaves beneath ;
Though a few years since, ah ! too well known,
The monster swallow'd a populous town—

SUB-CHORUS OF OCEANIDES.

To save it from Ætna's breath !

SUB-CHORUS THE THIRD.

Our home is in the red rock—
    Green rock—
    Grey rock—

Grassy bank, or the mountain side,
　With lava-stones abounding,
　Land and sea-beasts' bones surrounding,
We wall out the wind and the tide.

Our food has been the dog's food—
　　　Hawk's food—
　　　Hog's food—
But dainties we soon shall crunch and quaff;
　With the Titan's gift this morning,
　New years of strength adorning,
At Nature's old convulsions we shall laugh.

CHORUS.

See! see! see!
Dread Shapes and Portents of calamity!
A rush—a rushing through the clouds!
　Which heave and burst and fly,
　　And now are driven
　Athwart the Olympian Heaven,
In broken shades and adverse forms.
　Unlike all natural storms,
As though invisible demi-gods, in crowds,
　Fled in their wild dismays
　Before the javelin rays
　　Of Helios' car,—
Assaulted on his never-changing ways!

SUB-CHORUS OF OCEANIDES.

See! see! see!
A meteor dashes suddenly,
　Aslant from out the air,
Towards earth!—but lo! it vanishes in air!
　And horrid Shadows now,
　Stream in a threatening row,
　As if to bar and scare
Descent, and passage through——

CHORUS.

Despair! despair!
Prometheus fails!—behold his arm
Battling and breaking through the storm!
Four blasts converging, like cross seas,
And needing, to repel all these,
The form of the Hekatoncheires!
Yet see! he issues, swathed in conflicting glooms!
And downward comes,
Leaping and bounding,
From black cloud-ledges, broken stair by stair,
'Midst the Four Winds, resounding,
And wrestling still
Against his course—
Hissing, and yelling shrill;
Now hollow and hoarse,—
Striving to tear,
And straining out to frightful points his hair!

ECHO.

In the heavens afar,
'Midst dark flying clouds, I hear the war,
The scream and the jar,
The hiss and the roar,—
The swinging and whirling,
Wild winging and swirling,
The rents—the combining,
The knots—the entwining,
That, strangling, close binds,
And deafens and blinds,—
'Tis the wrestling of the Winds!

CHORUS.

Once more! once more in sight!
He plunges down the surging height!
Again assaulting Shades surround,
And hide the Titan from our view;

Yet downwards tow'rds this rocky ground
He surely comes, by fall or bound ;
And now he re-appears in swarthy hue,
   'Midst the Winds, howling bleak,
   And on the mountain's topmost peak
     His feet alight !
Down, down he comes in battling flight,
   And fainting, as from some death blow—
Smitten by bolts of Zeus, or Ætna's rocky balls—
Prone at the mountain's foot our Champion falls !

SUB-CHORUS OF OCEANIDES.

[*With cithara and phormynx.*]

Behold his reddened limbs outlaid !
Scorch'd, like the clay whereof he made
The first Man, and Man's mind with golden beams arrayed !

But now he lies, a giant heap,
In death-trance, or in dying sleep,
And o'er his stone-carv'd face, his massive locks fall deep !

CHORUS.

Hath he obtained the wondrous prize ?
For, lying here, with granite-lidded eyes,
We fear it 'bodes us evil destinies !

SUB-CHORUS OF OCEANIDES.

His lips move—but no sound we hear !
Approach him softly !—near—more near.

CHORUS.

Again his lips essay to speak—
And one large tear rolls down his umber'd cheek !
Listen ! Oh, listen to his words,
Faint as Æolia's dying chords !

PROMETHEUS.
Rejoice !

CHORUS.

He lives !—the Titan cannot die,
But on the earth may passive lie,—
Alas ! throughout eternity !

PROMETHEUS.

Rejoice !

CHORUS.

He speaks ! he hath escaped the blasting rays
Of the Sun's chariot, and the scathing blaze
From wrathful Zeus!—but into sudden night
His daring torch was dashed.

SUB-CHORUS OF OCEANIDES.

But lo ! how bright
Yon hollow reed doth trembling hold
The prize, of wonders manifold,
Preserved !—the spark intensely white,
Fresh from the sacred fount of Life and Light !

CHORUS.

Oh, Earth ring forth your gladness !
Rejoice ye seas and skies !
No more of want, of ignorance, and sadness—
Prometheus from the ground doth rise !

SUB-CHORUS OF OCEANIDES.

Hark ! hark !—Oh, listen to the sound
Of silver trumpets under ground !
Athena bids all things that be,
Thrill to that march of Victory !

PROMETHEUS.

Now may ye fabricate all implements
For agriculture, home-use, and for building

Houses and ships and temples to the Gods ;
Learning all arts to make earth habitable,
Man's life to cherish, and prolong in years,
Rendering his path more flowery and complete,
So that he may look upward evermore,
Blessing the Gods for all things.   But, indeed,
Having this gift I bring, do not, misjudging,
Sink into indolence and unfounded hopes,
From this bright, dangerous servant, but exert
All faculties for its appropriate use.

CHORUS.
To thee—and all this—we devote ourselves.

PROMETHEUS.
Sea-coasts and inland countries ye shall learn,
And how to find each spot with least delay—
To trace, re-trace, and never to be lost ;
As steers the bird his voyage through the air—
Clear as the local memories of a horse,
Direct as points the compass in his brain ;
Gifts of their natures, but which man, by art,
Will, in due time, acquire.   In every clime—
On land, or sea, a new friend shall he find :
Nipped by white death in frozen tracks, or lost
In maddening woods, man lights a fire, and smiles !
These things I well foresee—some near at hand—
Some, after years—some, in remoter ages,
And some, which ye may have, but never hold—
Instincts and revelations snatched away—
Material good made perfect, and o'erthrown,
And man roll'd back into a barbarous time,
Thence to begin again.   It may be so.

CHORUS.
O, cease Prometheus—far too wise—
These melancholy prophecies !

PROMETHEUS.

Meantime, ye children of the present hour,
Enjoy it, and employ it for the best,
And, in my absence, think that I am near,
E'en though ye never should behold me more,
Since Fate will not permit that I should tarry
Among ye long.   My path of operation,
E'en half its scope, comes to the precipice.

ECHO.

" To the precipice !"

SUB-CHORUS THE FIRST.

Hark ! Echo calls !

SUB-CHORUS THE SECOND.

Lost on the distant waves !

SUB-CHORUS THE THIRD.

Among the island's founts and falls,
        Or sea-weed caves !

CHORUS.

O Zeus ! what words doth Echo now repeat
        From the remote dark air,
        Flushing with fitful glare,
While black clouds open round the Thron'd One's feet !

ECHO.

" Accomplished ! "

CHORUS.

Hark ! from Mount Ida's sky !

ECHO.

" Descended with the prize ! "

CHORUS.

Where shall we fly !
Yes, 'tis the voice of Zeus which Echo brings
On her invisible wings !
Appalling—freezing—clear, not loud—
From yonder scudding rack of ghastly cloud !

ECHO.

" Prometheus ! "

SUB-CHORUS OF OCEANIDES.

Lo ! the words of Zeus !

ECHO.

" Prometheus !"

PROMETHEUS.

Speak !—he knows his destiny

CHORUS.

Where shall we fly ?
Where darkly lie ?—
Oh, spare !—
What depth of deepest shade
Can blot us from thine Eye !
Oh, spare !
Oh, spare, dread Zeus ! the creatures thou hast made !

ECHO.

" Prometheus ! son of fallen Iapetus !
    " The son of Ouranos !—the son of Gæa !—son
    " Of Chaos !—
    " Thou hast robbed the eternal Fountain,
    " Essence, and spirit
    " Of Life—the life of all Heaven's reigning Gods—
    " All Gods that yet may reign—
    " And life of all the things that creep on earth,

" Or yet may creep, swim, walk, or fly, or feel—
" And brought it down, in madness, to redeem
" Fallen man !"

PROMETHEUS.

This service have I done the race.

ECHO.

" Rash Titan !—
" Foreknowledge is not knowledge of the Present,
" In all its forms and necessary grades
" Through centuries.   I reign.   Take thy reward !"

PROMETHEUS.

Foreknowledge sculptures fortitude, in minds
Worthy to hold foreknowledge.

CHORUS.

Reigning Zeus !
Thou Present God !—spare us !—we are innocent !
It was the Titan-god, Prometheus,
Who braved thy bolts omnipotent !
We had no mad intent—
No thought—no hope—
No wish to enlarge our scope,—
But with our abject lot we were content,
Born, as we were, in that low element !
And if aught more we e'er desired,
It was because we were inspired
By the fall'n Titan's son,
Who of himself hath done—
By his own plan—
His views of God and man—
This dreadful deed, wherewith our hearts were fired !

SUB-CHORUS OF OCEANIDES.

Dark clouds close in the skies,—
And far-off Echo speaks no more ; but we,

With shame cast down our sea-green eyes,
At your ungrateful falsity !

SUB-CHORUS THE FIRST.

We spake the truth.

SUB-CHORUS THE SECOND.

Though 'twas not brave
Ourselves to save,
Thrusting our Champion underneath the wave !

SUB-CHORUS THE THIRD.

Who comes ?
Oh, be still !
'Tis the great Iron-hand !
His furrow'd brow glooms,
Zeus' wrath to fulfil,
And trample us into the sand !
O, spare ! we are innocent !—all has been done
By the Titan, Prometheus—standing alone !

HEPHAISTOS.

As all will stand alone among mankind
After such dangerous service.   I am come—
Not without pain, Prometheus—being sent—
And pain from several causes.   I am lame—
But that is not the worst of all I feel—
Only I do not deem it wise to speak
What I fain would ;—unnecessary words
To one who knows.   But, for these Islanders—
This human race—all those who stand around,
Trembling and shuffling, both in feet and mind—
Yes, all of these, except great Ocean's Daughters,
Who are most constant in their love to thee,—
Did I not tell thee, Titan, to thy front
And tower-skull pitch of knowledge, that thy work

And its results, were prodigally spent
Upon a selfish and ungrateful herd ?

PROMETHEUS.

To know all, is to forgive.

HEPHAISTOS.

But I, indeed,
Have not so full a knowledge, and I do not,
In any one respect forgive this herd.

SUB-CHORUS THE THIRD.

What should we know of these great dreams ?
At all new things we gape, surprised !
If good for us—or worst, or best,
O, forge-black God, we know no test !
When from above a sudden wonder gleams,
We start up, all dismayed and paralysed,
While our breast heaves,
Like to some lonely bird, when through the leaves,
A human face looks in upon her nest !

CHORUS.

We thought the hour was come for us to die !
At certain times man is not half himself !
It was not we who spake—it was our fear !

PROMETHEUS.

Like death-bed babblings, when a man hath lost
His nerves and steady sense, and his poor brain
Spins off the melting pictures of the past—
Into wild darkness.   All men fear to die :
'Tis wrong, yet reasonable.   Comfort ye, my sons,
With recollection of your strongest hours,
And loftiest thoughts.

CHORUS.

Believe, Prometheus, what we said
Broke from us—as from men half dead !

Sub-Chorus the First.

'Tis mid-day now—yet Heaven grows dark !
The Sun rolls on behind, in gloom ;
Some Fury, like a winged shark,
  Seems coming with a dreadful doom !

Chorus.

It passes onward—but for whom ?

Choragus.

What are those Figures standing in the shadow
Of overhanging rocks ?—themselves like rocks—
Or, are they also, shadows?

Hephaistos.

Strength and Force !
They come to bear away Prometheus !

Chorus.

Oh, God of Day !
Take back the glorious prize,
Won by the Titan from thy mourning skies !
And let us, wretched, on this barren shore,
Remain as hopeless as before !

Hephaistos.

Your right minds come too late for gratitude,—
A curse that will beset ye to the end.
Now screams the eagle for your champion's heart !

Sub-Chorus of Oceanides.

The fangs may rend, the hailstorm freeze ;
  He will endure for future fruit,
And, silent as the growth of trees,
  Believe in Sun-light, and a root !

D

HEPHAISTOS.

Prometheus ! I must bear thee far away,
To centuries of torture—as thou know'st—
Bound on the top of Caucasus, whose white horror
Scowls o'er the loftiest Hyperborean peaks.

SUB-CHORUS OF OCEANIDES.

All graceful are the flowers
    At the bottom of the sea,
And the gleaming Ghosts and Shadows,
    That, dilating, come—and flee !
But the caves of black coral,
    And profoundest depths of gloom,
We will seek—and not speak—
    But think Curses on this doom !

HEPHAISTOS.

Those who can do nought else, may curse their fill.
The reign of the Ouranidai is no more :
They are but Clouds enthroned in a crazy brain.

SUB-CHORUS OF OCEANIDES.

We wander through the waves
    And the coral caves
        Of Tethys ;
O'er the sands, and salt strands,
    And the weedy rocks of Metis ;
To the groves and alcoves,
    Where the Oread's seat is,
And the Syrens chaunt our sacred theme !

But each morn, isles of spawn
    In the east lie burning,
It ever brings to mind,
    With its glories returning,

Our fathers' lost thrones—
>> Till, with mad passion yearning,
We plunge to our deep, deep Dream !

HEPHAISTOS.

It is impossible to hear plants grow,
Or the Hours move ; nor can I hear ye rave—
But I can see ye raving.   Plunge deep down—
This Dynasty is lasting.   Strength, and Force !
Wake from your pedestals among those rocks,
And lead the way to Scythia's frozen wilds !

PROMETHEUS.

Daughters of Ocean !—friends at worst of seasons,
True hearts, unchanging when all others fail—
Farewell !   And you, my sons, of mortal mould,—
True also in the centre of your hearts—
Where all, indeed, are true, in their degree—
Treasure my gift—remember well my words,
And teach yourselves by labour ; offering prayers
To the just Gods ; and, more especially,
Athena and Hephaistos ; Aphrodite
(Profound her worship as the source of life)
At fitting seasons ; and Apollo always,
As God of many gracious arts and aims,—
Who, with Hephaistos and my brother, Helios,
Present the triune master-spirit—Fire !

SUB-CHORUS OF OCEANIDES.

Earth ! Heaven ! and Poesy !
We are all handmaids to the three,
And of the Champion of Humanity !

HEPHAISTOS.

Again the eagle screams !   It must be done.

SUB-CHORUS OF OCEANIDES.

O, Helios !—Athena,
Adored by the Titan !
O, Phoibos-Apollo !
And thou, dread Hephaistos,
Not willingly coming
From white Aphrodite !
We shriek, O remember
Heaven's earliest Throned-Ones—
The great Ouranidai !
Behold ! led to torture,
Through ages uncounted,
Their noblest Descendant !

HEPHAISTOS.

Titan, while honoring thee, I well remember
Thy race, and hold in reasonable dread
Thy possible acts.   Iapetus lies prone ;
Typhon, a monstrous effigy of coal—
Titans and Giants roll in Tartarus,
With chain and bolt of thrice-clamped manacles,
'Neath rocks which Chaos might himself approve ;
But thou, indeed, with a spear-brandishing hand,
And sun-distorting shield of polished brass—
Besides thy subtle counsels, arts, and skill—
May'st lead new wars for an Olympian Throne !

SUB-CHORUS OF OCEANIDES.

He answers not, in his disdain ;
He had no thought to war, or reign ;
Mankind alone engaged that earth-enfolding brain

HEPHAISTOS.

Wherefore, Prometheus, son of Iapetus—
The son of Ouranos—son of Gæa—son

Of Chaos—lineage highest, *but* the foe
Of Zeus !—thy torturing doom through centuries,
Is fixed.

CHORUS.

Ai ! ai ! ai !

PROMETHEUS.

I have done my work.

HEPHAISTOS.

On, now, to Caucasus !

SUB-CHORUS OF OCEANIDES.

We shall be there,
With frost-white flowers and flowing hair,
By tear, and tender sigh to cheer,
And ever bear thee company
In that congealing air !
Thy brow shall wear a pyracanthine wreath,
Above the icy glare of Fate, and idiot Death!

CHORUS.

Ai ! ai ! ai !

ECHO.

" Valiant ! valiant ! "

CHORUS.

Behold, the chariot of the Sun breaks forth,
Above our heads !
And on the all-reviving Earth
Its full meridian' fulgence sheds !
Through yonder glaring break
The Voice of Helios spake !
See ! see ! the tightened reign !
List to the far-off Voice, again !

Echo.

"Valiant Prometheus !
"Titan !
"Brother !
" Heaven—Earth—and Ocean —
" Night—starry Mother !
" Greet thee, this day ! "

Chorus.

Onward away ! away his steeds,
   Mad with the momentary pause,
     Plunge through the scattered clouds !—
      Helios !
The East, at heart, exults and bleeds
   In crimson founts and purpling flaws,
     Seen through the flying vapoury shrouds !—
      Helios !
The wind flares back his blazing hair !
   Away he whirls !—a new-born sphere !
'Midst rolling swathes of stormy gold—
     Fold over-running fold,
     Divided rock, and torn-up dell,
     Temple, and fallen citadel,
      Of architectural Air—
     In one far-radiating glare
The exalted form, and chariot, disappear !
     All but the uprais'd guiding hand,
And dizzy, whitening wheel, half-seen, below !

Choragus.

He's gone !—again on earth we stand !
   But not with our old wants and woe :
For though the gorgeous billows close behind
   That life-creating car—while our redeemer,
     Promethens,

Is borne to torture in captivity,
    On hell-surpassing Caucasus,—
Yet hath he left the seeds of a great mind,
    To germinate through ages slow,
        And flourish in futurity,—
Realized visions of the martyr'd dreamer!
        For all things now,
    To us poor mortals, rich in hope,
        Whom also faith and love inspire,
Are placed within our work's expanding scope,
    By the pure gift of Fire!

Edmonston and Douglas, Edinburgh

www.ingramcontent.com/pod-product-compliance
Lightning Source LLC
Chambersburg PA
CBHW022157020726
47496CB00008B/2755